*M*eg **March** is the perfect young lady. Her gracious manners and sweet personality make her very popular at school. So when Meg is invited to Mary Howe's fancy picnic, she is eager to go. Nothing her tomboy sister, Jo, says against snobbish Mary Howe changes Meg's mind. Meg claims Jo is just jealous because she wasn't invited too. But on the big day, the March parents are visiting friends and the housekeeper is called away on an emergency. Meg knows she should stay home to watch over her younger sisters—even if it means not going to the picnic. Still . . . Meg doesn't want to miss the fun and, forgetting her manners, does something that turns the picnic into an unforgettable afternoon.

PORTRAITS
of LITTLE WOMEN
Meg's Story

Don't miss any of the
Portraits of Little Women

Meg's Story

Jo's Story

Beth's Story

Amy's Story

PORTRAITS
of LITTLE WOMEN
Meg's Story

Susan Beth Pfeffer

S

DELACORTE PRESS

FOR TOM ARIS

Published by
Delacorte Press
Bantam Doubleday Dell Publishing Group, Inc.
1540 Broadway
New York, New York 10036

Library of Congress Cataloging-in-Publication Data
Pfeffer, Susan Beth.
  Portraits of Little Women, Meg's story/Susan Beth Pfeffer.
    p.   cm.
  Based on characters found in Louisa May Alcott's Little Women.
  Summary: When ten-year-old Meg receives an invitation to a friend's
picnic but Jo does not, Meg must decide whether to decline out of
loyalty to her sister or to follow her heart and attend.
  ISBN 0-385-32520-7
  [1. Family life—Fiction.   2. Sisters—Fiction.   3. Picnicking—Fiction.]
I. Alcott, Louisa May, 1832–1888. Little Women.   II. Title.
PZ7.P44855Po   1997
[Fic]—dc21   97-6141
                                                                CIP
                                                                 AC

The text of this book is set in 13-point Cochin.

Cover and text design by Patrice Sheridan
Cover illustration copyright © 1997 by Lori Earley
Text illustrations copyright © 1997 by Marcy Ramsey
Activities illustrations copyright © 1997 by Laura Maestro

Manufactured in the United States of America

November 1997

10   9   8   7   6   5

BVG

CONTENTS

I. Meg's Story   1

II. Activities
   Strawberry Shortcake Recipe   75
   Drawstring Bag Craft Project   77

III. Sneak Peek Chapters
   Jo's Story   85
   Beth's Story   89
   Amy's Story   96

PORTRAITS
of LITTLE WOMEN

Meg's Story

CHAPTER 1

*M*eg March looked at her slate and sighed. Would the school day never end?

Ordinarily Meg enjoyed school. She loved to read, and she liked history as well. Her family was a part of American history. Two of her great-grandfathers had fought in the American Revolution. Even arithmetic, which was what her class was supposed to be working on just then, could be interesting.

But not on the first day of June. Not when the sun was shining and the classroom, which had been cold all winter long, was warm enough to encourage dozing. Not when she and her sisters were halfway through their most recent play, which would, of course, star Meg and Jo. Beth had agreed to play the piano for the play, and Amy was now old enough to memorize lines and could be given small parts to perform. It was certain to be their best production ever.

And the day was so lovely that when they got home, they could work on the play in the garden. So why wouldn't the school day end?

Meg looked quickly toward Jo's seat. Jo was a year younger, and they were in the same classroom. Beth and Amy were in a classroom for younger children. Meg wondered if they were as impatient as she was for lessons to be over. Jo was, she knew, but Jo was impatient about everything.

Meg feared she might explode, but fortunately the bell rang and the teacher dismissed the class. Meg noticed that he too seemed relieved, and she supposed it couldn't be fun to rein in the spirits of twenty-five children aged nine through eleven on a beautiful afternoon in June. Her parents frequently told her to be considerate of the feelings of others. Meg was pleased with herself that she cared about her teacher's feelings. She doubted Jo thought of him at all.

In fact, Jo had already escaped from the school by the time Meg reached the front door. Meg waited a moment, until Beth and Amy appeared, and then they walked out together. Jo, she noted, was racing with some of the boys from their class. Jo was the best runner in their class, and she never minded letting the boys know that.

"Jo isn't very ladylike," Amy said as they watched their sister win yet another race.

"Jo isn't ladylike at all," replied Meg.

"But you're a lady, Meg," said Beth.

"I'm more of one than Jo, but not nearly as much of one as Amy," Meg replied with a laugh.

"You can laugh," Amy said, "but I intend to marry great wealth someday, and I'll be more of a lady than anybody else in this town has ever been."

"Concord has many ladies," Beth said.

"Doesn't it, Meg? Aunt March is a lady. And Marmee is the best lady of all."

"Amy means the kind of lady who wears silks and laces all the time," Meg said. "And doesn't make do with mended calicoes."

"You have no right to complain," said Amy. "I have it worst of all. Practically every dress I've ever owned you wore once, then Jo and then Beth. It wouldn't be so bad if it were just you, or even you and Beth. But Jo rips everything, and I spend half my life in patches." She looked so mournful that Meg burst out laughing again.

"Meg March! Wait for me!"

Meg turned around and saw Mary Howe calling for her. Mary was in the same class as Meg and Jo. And she was definitely Amy's idea of a lady. It was clear that Mary had never worn a patched piece of clothing in her life.

"Meg, I want to speak to you," Mary said as she joined the March sisters.

"Certainly, Mary," said Meg. Beth, always shy, was hiding as best she could behind Meg.

4

Amy was staring straight at Mary, drinking in the details of Mary's perfect blue dress and its white lace collar.

"I'm having a picnic on Saturday," Mary announced. "My brother, Willie, and I. Mama said I could invite three girls and Willie could invite three boys. Willie's asked Freddie and James and George. I've asked Priscilla Browne and Sallie Gardiner and now I'm asking you. Do say you'll come. Sallie Gardiner has often said it's not your fault your family has so little money, and I agree. You're quite the nicest girl in our class, and very ladylike in spite of your family's straits."

"Why, thank you," Meg said. "A picnic sounds lovely."

"It will be," said Mary. "We'll play games and eat ice cream and have the most wonderful time."

"I'll have to ask my mother first," Meg said. "But if she says I may, I'd love to attend your picnic."

"I'm so glad," Mary said. "Please tell your mother that my mother thinks she is the most splendid lady. Tell me tomorrow whether you can come. The picnic will be at one o'clock on Saturday. I do hope you'll attend." She took Meg's hand and gave it an affectionate squeeze, then walked away to join her brother, Willie.

Meg was so delighted, she laughed out loud with joy.

CHAPTER 2

"*A* picnic with ice cream," Amy said once Mary had left. "Oh, Meg. How perfectly wonderful."

"You see, Amy," Beth said, "the Howes know that Marmee is a great lady. And they think you are too, Meg. You're lady enough to be invited to their picnic."

"I do try hard to be a lady," Meg said. "It would be easier, I know, if Father still had some money."

"Jo could have all the money in the world and she'd never be a lady," said Amy. "And I could have none, and everyone would still be able to tell that I was one. Although I'll never have no money."

"What about me?" Beth asked. "Am I a lady?"

Meg looked down at her shy little sister. "You are a perfect lady," she said. "Just as Marmee is. A true lady cares for others even more than she cares for herself."

"I care for others too," Amy said. "I just care for silks and lace as well."

Meg gave each of her two younger sisters an embrace. "We are all ladies," she said. "And Jo will be content being a perfect gentleman."

"What's that you're saying about me?" Jo asked, running straight into the path of her sisters.

"That we're all ladies," replied Amy. "Except for you, Jo."

"As though I care about frills and fripperies," Jo said. "I'm going to be a great writer. And great writers are devoted to their art. They don't care a fig about society."

"Don't use slang," Meg said, although Jo

8

always did, and Meg supposed she always would.

"I'll use slang if I want to," Jo said. "I like slang. And I like running too, so don't lecture me about that either."

"I have no intention of lecturing you about anything," Meg said. "You're old enough to know what you should and shouldn't do."

"Then why did you tell me not to use slang?"

"That wasn't a lecture," said Beth. "That was a command."

"And a none too successful one," admitted Meg. "Very well, Jo. Be rough and boyish if you like."

"And I do like," Jo said. "There are quite enough ladies in this family as it is. It's bad enough I have to be a girl. I refuse to be a little prissy one, like that Mary Howe I saw you talking to."

"There's nothing wrong with Mary Howe," Meg said. "She comes from one of the best families in Massachusetts. And I've noticed you playing with Willie Howe often enough."

"Willie's all right," Jo said. "Although I beat him every time we race. But Mary's just the kind of girl I loathe, full of airs and acting so dainty all the time. I'll say this for you, Meg. You may talk about being a lady and tell me not to use slang, but at least you're not dainty."

Meg wasn't sure that she didn't want to be dainty. She knew that she and Jo would never agree on many things. But she also knew that Jo was truthful and loving and more fun than anybody else.

"I think it must be wonderful to be dainty," Amy said. "And I'm sure I'd be far more dainty if Jo hadn't dropped me as a baby and flattened my poor nose."

"You're lucky I didn't flatten your poor head," Jo said. "I know I've been tempted to often enough."

"Josephine March!" Amy cried. "What a terrible thing to say."

"It was, Jo," said Meg.

"I'm sorry, then," Jo replied. "But the way Amy complains about that nose of hers, you'd

11

think I'd sinned against all humanity by dropping her that one time."

"If all humanity had a nose like mine, I'm sure they'd feel the same way I do," said Amy. "And it's just because Meg is a lady, all proper and fine the way a lady should be, that Mary Howe invited her to her picnic and not you."

"What's this about a picnic?" asked Jo.

"It's on Saturday," Meg said. "And I'm sure Mary would have liked to ask you, but her mother gave her permission to ask only three girls. And Willie can ask three boys. It's Willie you play with, and he can't ask you because you're a girl. Mary asked Priscilla and Sallie and me."

"Because they're all true ladies," Amy said, "who don't use slang and tear their dresses and threaten to flatten the heads of their baby sisters."

"Of course you won't go," Jo said to Meg, ignoring Amy, as she often tried to do.

"And why not?" asked Meg.

"Because Mary slighted me," Jo said. "She could have asked me as well as you and not have invited Priscilla or Sallie."

"And why should she have done that?" Meg demanded. "Priscilla and Sallie are her friends. You've never said a good word about Mary. You were making fun of her just now until you heard about the picnic."

"That's not the point," said Jo. "The point is family comes first. And since I have been slighted, you owe it to the honor of the March family to refuse to attend Mary's picnic."

"I owe the honor of the March family no such thing," declared Meg. "I'm the sort of girl Mary likes, so naturally she invited me. If you made just a little effort to be more ladylike, then other girls would invite you to their picnics and parties. You've brought this on yourself, Jo, and don't expect me to sacrifice my happiness for your silly pride."

"Very well," Jo said. "From now on, play with Mary and her friends and don't bother with me."

"Jo," Beth said, "don't be angry at Meg's good fortune."

"I'll be angry if I want," Jo said.

"And so will I," Meg said.

And it was four unhappy sisters who walked back to the March home together.

CHAPTER 3

"*M*armee, Marmee!" Jo cried. "Meg's been invited to a picnic and I haven't and she doesn't love me enough to refuse to go."

"And why should I?" demanded Meg. "Beth and Amy weren't invited either, and they're not angry."

"They're babies," replied Jo.

"I'm no baby," Amy said. "I'm more of a lady than you'll ever be."

"Girls, girls," their mother said. "Be quiet. You know I won't listen to any of you when you shout in that manner."

"I'm sorry, Marmee," Meg said. "It's just

15

that Jo is choosing to ruin the most perfect day. She's selfish and mean and I don't see any reason why I should have to give up the one good thing that's ever happened to me just to make her happy."

"*I'm* selfish and mean?" exploded Jo. "I'm not the one who chooses to play with nasty little ladies like Mary Howe."

"What did I just say about how you should speak?" asked Marmee.

"That we should be quiet," Beth said. "I'm trying to be quiet, Marmee."

"And a fine job you're doing of it," her mother said, giving Beth a hug. "Now, Meg. You speak first. Tell me just what has happened. And leave out all the nasty tones and accusations."

"I will, Marmee," Meg promised. "Mary Howe invited me to a picnic at her house on Saturday. I told her I'd ask you, and if you said yes, then I'd be happy to attend. That's all."

"That is not all!" cried Jo. "She didn't invite me. She invited Meg and Priscilla Browne and

16

Sallie Gardiner and not me. And Meg thinks it's perfectly fine to go, even though the honor of the entire March family has been besmirched."

"You see, Marmee?" Meg said. "That's what I've had to put up with the entire walk home from school. It's Jo's own fault she wasn't asked. Mary specifically said she was inviting me because I was a lady. She said her mother thinks you're a great lady, Marmee. Even though . . ." And then Meg's firm voice faltered.

"Even though what?" asked Marmee.

"Even though we don't have money," Amy finished for Meg. "Although Jo could be rich as Midas and she still wouldn't be a lady."

"Did Mary say that as well?" Jo asked.

"No, I did," Amy said.

"Mary didn't mention Jo at all, Marmee," Meg said. "She said I was a lady and her mother held you in the highest esteem, and I don't see how that could be bad. And if Jo chooses to play with boys and get dirty all the time, then that's her choice and I shouldn't be punished for it."

"Nobody has said anything about punishment," said Marmee. "Jo, you are rough and wild and you almost never play with girls other than your sisters. Why do you think Mary should have invited you to her picnic?"

"Because she invited Meg," Jo said. "And it isn't fair Meg got invited and I didn't."

"Someday a man will fall in love with Meg and ask her to marry him," said Marmee. "Would you think it unfair if he didn't ask you as well?"

All the girls but Jo laughed at the idea. "It's not the same thing," Jo said. "A man can't have two wives. But Mary can certainly have two Marches."

"She can't, Marmee," said Meg. "Mrs. Howe told Mary she could invite three girls. Not three girls and their sisters. Naturally she invited Priscilla and Sallie. Priscilla and Sallie and Mary are friends. I'm lucky Mary thought to invite me as well."

"And do you like Mary?" Marmee asked.

"Yes, I do," Meg said. "She has such pretty dresses and so many of them. And she never fights or acts rough. She's just the sort of lady you want us to be, Marmee."

"Tell me, Jo," said Marmee. "Do you like Mary?"

"Not a bit," Jo replied. "She's full of airs."

"If you don't like her, Jo, then I'm sure you can understand why she might not like you," Marmee said. "And if she and Meg do like each other, then it seems most reasonable to me that Meg would be invited to the picnic. I want my daughters to be loving and caring sisters, but they are individuals and have the right to lead their own lives and make their own friendships. You wouldn't expect Meg to play your sorts of games, now, would you, Jo?"

"That's her choice," Jo grumbled. "She could race and play hoops if she wanted."

"And if she didn't want to but did it anyway, how would you feel?" Marmee asked.

"I'd feel she was being foolish," Jo said. "Pretending to be someone she wasn't."

Marmee gave Jo a hug. "That is one sin you'll never commit," she said. "And because you are so honest with yourself, Jo, I'm sure you know why it's right for Meg to accept Mary's invitation."

Jo scowled. "I suppose," she said. "Meg will go and play with Mary and Priscilla and Sallie. They'll sew dainty things for their dolls and be ever so careful not to get dirty. But I wish I could be there to play with Willie and his friends. It's not fair he can only ask boys. I'm sure if he could, he would ask me."

"It may seem unfair to you," Marmee said, "but that is what Mrs. Howe thinks best. And we must respect her wishes just as much as we respect Mary's."

"I'll have a picnic someday, Jo," Beth said. "And you'll be the very first person I'll invite."

"And someday I'll have a grand ball," Amy said. "And I'll invite you too, Jo."

"But not first, I wager," said Jo.

Amy looked dreamy. "I shall invite all the

crowned heads of Europe first," she said. "And the President of the United States and the governor of Massachusetts. And Marmee and Father, and Meg and Beth and you."

"Must I go?" Beth asked. "I'm sure I wouldn't know what to say to all those crowned heads."

"We'll worry about that when the time comes," Marmee declared. "In the meantime, there's a beautiful June afternoon going to waste with all these quarrels."

"You're right," Jo said. "And Meg and I have a play to stage. Come, Meg. Our play needs a lady for its heroine." She grabbed her sister's hand and pulled her toward the door.

"Jo!" Meg protested, but she was laughing. It was true Jo grew dark as a thundercloud sometimes, but she became sunny nearly as fast. With Jo, you were never bored.

CHAPTER 4

The girls worked on their play until it was time for supper. Jo praised Meg to the skies for her acting and marveled at how well Amy, who had just learned to read, could remember her lines. Beth, who sang the tunes she would be playing on the piano, was agreed by all to have a voice as sweet as an angel's. And each of the sisters, in turn, told Jo how exciting her play was. By afternoon's end, they were four sisters united forever.

"My little women seem unusually contented tonight," their father said after supper that evening.

His daughters laughed out loud. "You should have seen us earlier today," said Jo.

"No, you shouldn't have," Meg said.

"Meg's invited to a picnic," Amy said. "Saturday afternoon. With ice cream."

"Ice cream?" Father asked. "That sounds quite wonderful. Your mother and I will be making a social call of our own Saturday afternoon. We've been invited, my dear, to visit the Emersons."

"I will enjoy that," Marmee said. "Jo, you must think of something entertaining for you and Beth and Amy to do. Perhaps Hannah can make a picnic lunch and you could eat it in the garden."

"Could we, Marmee?" Beth asked. "That sounds so nice."

"There won't be bugs, will there?" Amy asked. "I hate bugs."

"If there are any, I'll crush them for you," Jo said. "We'll pretend they're the British invading our shores and we alone can keep them from conquest."

"Jo makes a game of everything," Beth said. "I think we'll probably have more fun than Meg will at her picnic."

For a moment, Meg thought the same. But then she remembered the ice cream and the pretty things Mary owned and decided she'd rather go to Mary's picnic. Besides, she'd fought so hard to be allowed to attend.

"We shall all have a fine time of it Saturday," Father said. "I think that calls for a song. Bethy, would you play the piano for us? You're the only one who can make that old thing sing."

"I'd love to, Father," Beth said. Playing the piano was her one true joy and the only talent she was happy to show off. "What do you care to hear?"

"Something jolly," her father replied. "Some of those Stephen Foster songs we all so enjoy singing."

Beth found the book of music and opened it to "Oh, Susanna." Soon the whole family was singing the comical lyrics together.

"This is my favorite song!" cried Amy, and as the family harmonized, she danced a little jig to show her pleasure.

Meg looked at her family and knew herself to be the luckiest girl in all of Massachusetts.

CHAPTER 5

"Have a good afternoon, girls," Marmee said as she and Father prepared to leave. "Meg, be a good guest at the Howes'. Don't overstay your welcome. Father and I should be back before nightfall. Don't squabble among yourselves, and obey Hannah."

"We will, Marmee," her daughters promised. They watched as their parents began the long walk to the Emerson house.

"I hope it doesn't rain on our picnic," Amy said, casting an anxious look at the sky. There were a few dark clouds looming overhead.

"If it does, what of it?" said Jo. "We'll simply move the picnic indoors."

"Don't even speak of rain," said Meg. She had spent the week in a blaze of anticipation, barely concentrating on her schoolwork or her tasks at home. "It simply mustn't rain."

"Then it won't," Beth said, and she sounded so definite about it that they all laughed.

"Help me decide what books to take to the picnic," Jo said to Meg. "Our picnic will feature Miss Josephine March and her recitations."

"I want Meg to help me find my pencils," Amy said. "I'm going to draw the most beautiful pictures while Jo reads."

"I need Meg to help me choose which doll to take to the picnic," said Beth. "Martha has been my best-behaved dolly all week, but poor Emma is still recovering from Jo's pulling her arm off and could use a special treat."

"Why not take both?" Meg suggested. "Neither one of them will eat very much."

"Do you think?" Beth asked. "Thank you, Meg. That's a wonderful solution."

"I never meant to pull Emma's arm off," Jo grumbled as she glanced about her room, looking for the appropriate reading matter for a picnic. "Somehow she ended up on my writing papers, and when I picked her up, her arm fell off."

"I don't blame you," Beth said. "And neither does Emma. But it is hard on a doll to lose her right arm."

"I imagine so," Meg said. "And think of what a treat it will be for her to be outdoors this afternoon. Just keep Jo away from her."

"I promise to go nowhere near Emma," Jo said. "Or well-behaved Martha either."

"I wish I had a pastel set," said Amy. "All the best artists have pastel sets."

"I'm sure you will when you're a little older," Meg said. "I don't think Raphael or Rembrandt had pastel sets when they were six."

"Geniuses have to make do," Jo said. "Take my word for it."

"I will," Amy said. "But keep away from my arm, Jo. I need it for my art."

The girls were still laughing when Hannah, the housekeeper, called them downstairs.

"What is it?" Meg asked. Hannah sounded terribly upset, and it took a lot to upset her.

"It's my niece," Hannah said. "I just received a message that her baby is coming early. And with my poor sister dead, I'm the only mother that child has. I must go to be with her."

"We'll be fine, Hannah," Meg said. "You take care of your niece."

"I'll be back just as soon as I can," Hannah said. "Tell your mother what's happened when she gets home."

"We will," Meg promised.

Hannah ran out of the house. Her niece lived several miles away. Meg only hoped that by the time Hannah got there, everything would be all right.

CHAPTER 6

"We're all alone," Jo said. "We've never been all alone before."

"How long does it take to have a baby?" Amy asked.

"I'm not sure," Meg said. "An hour or two, I think."

"Suppose she's having the baby now," Jo said. "It'll take Hannah more than an hour to get there. Do you think she'll stay awhile, or just leave as soon as she sees the baby?"

"She'll stay," Meg said. "There are things you have to do when a baby's born. You have to wash things. And her niece won't feel like

30

cooking right away, so Hannah will probably stay to make everybody supper."

"She could be gone all day," Beth said. "Marmee and Father could get home before she does. And they won't be home until dark."

"It'll be all right," Meg said. "I'll be here to watch out for you."

"No, you won't," Amy said. "You're going to Mary Howe's picnic."

Meg couldn't believe she'd forgotten about that. "The picnic," she said. "Oh, dear."

"Don't you worry," Jo said. "You go to the picnic. I'll be in charge here."

Meg immediately thought about Emma the doll and her missing right arm. She knew it wasn't Jo's fault, but Jo could be rough sometimes. Meg also knew that Marmee would expect her to take care of her younger sisters, and that included Jo.

"No, I'm the oldest," said Meg. "I'll stay here and take care of you."

"But you want to go to the picnic," Beth said.

"That's all you've spoken about all week," said Amy.

"You *have* gone on about it," Jo said.

"Yes," Meg admitted. "Missing it will be a terrible disappointment." She sat down on Marmee's parlor chair and tried to feel like Marmee, all brave and noble and happy to make sacrifices. It didn't work.

"I'm disappointed too," Amy said. "I wanted to hear all about the picnic. I wanted to hear what Mary and Priscilla and Sallie wore and what kinds of elegant foods were served and how many servants the Howes have. I wanted to hear everything."

"Perhaps some other time," Meg said.

"But you simply can't not go," Beth said. "They'll wonder what happened to you."

"I should get a message to them," Meg said. "I suppose I could go over and explain the situation, and then come right back."

"We'd still be left alone then," Jo said.

"Then come with me!" Meg said, feeling exasperated by the whole situation. It was bad enough she was going to miss the picnic. She didn't need Jo and the others to act as though they'd be helpless without her.

"Could we really go with you?" Amy asked. "Do you think Mary would mind?"

"Mind what?" Meg asked.

"If we went on the picnic with you," Jo said. "Meg, that really is a capital idea."

"Don't use slang," Meg said, before she even realized what Jo had suggested. "You mean go with me to Mary's picnic?" She tried to keep the horror out of her voice.

"But that's what you just said," replied Amy. "That we should go with you. Oh, please, Meg. I should so love to see what everybody wears."

"And that way we wouldn't be alone," Jo said. "Mr. and Mrs. Howe would be there, and all of their servants. Marmee and Father would think it quite the safest place for us to be while Hannah's niece has her baby."

"Maybe Mary wouldn't like it," Beth said. "We weren't invited."

"That's right," Jo said. "*I* certainly wasn't." Her face grew dark and broody as she remembered the terrible slight.

Meg looked at her sisters. They were her responsibility until Hannah or Marmee came home. Jo couldn't be trusted with them, especially if she was going to be in one of her tempers. And though it was terribly unfair that Meg should be deprived of the Howes' picnic, Meg knew Beth was right as well. Only Meg had been invited. The Howes might not even have prepared enough food for all of them.

"We'll all have to stay here," Meg said with a sigh. "Jo, stop making such faces. I'm going to have just as bad a time as you."

"I don't understand," Amy said. "Meg, you're supposed to go on a picnic. And we're supposed to go on a picnic. Can't we just have our picnics at the same place?"

"We could do that," Jo said, and her face grew pleased and excited. "Amy could bring her pencils, and I could bring a book to recite from, and Beth could bring her dollies. Well, maybe just Emma. And we'll each bring our own food, so the Howes won't have to feed us. And you'll be right there, Meg, so you won't have to worry about us."

"And I'll get to see everything," Amy said. "All the beautiful dresses and servants."

"We'll keep very quiet," said Jo. "They'll hardly even know we're there."

"What do you think, Beth?" asked Meg.

"I think it would be all right," Beth replied, "if we really don't have to play with the others but can just sit and watch. I know Emma would enjoy it."

"Then that's the answer," Meg said. "But Jo, you must promise me not to fall into one of your tempers. And Beth, if by some chance someone speaks to you, you mustn't hide. You must respond politely. And Amy, do try not to be the center of attention. Just keep quietly to yourself."

"In other words, Amy and I are to keep our mouths closed, while Beth is to open hers," Jo said. "A hard order, Meg, but one we're all willing to try!"

CHAPTER 7

*M*eg knocked on the door of the Howes' house. It was a grand place, practically a mansion. A servant answered the door.

"Please announce that Meg March is here for the picnic," Meg squeaked. She had little experience with butlers and hoped she had said the right thing.

"Very well, miss," the butler replied.

In a moment Mrs. Howe was at the door. "Meg, dear, come in," she said. "You're the first to arrive. Mary is still dressing."

"I'm sorry I'm early," Meg said. "We had a

problem at home, and I needed to speak with you."

"Nothing serious, I hope," Mrs. Howe said. "Your parents and sisters are well?"

"Very well, thank you," Meg said. "But my parents are out visiting for the day, and our housekeeper was called away suddenly."

"And you have only the one servant?" Mrs. Howe said. "Ah, yes. Your family would find it hard to employ more than one."

Meg winced with embarrassment. "My sisters were planning a picnic of their own," she quickly said. "They've brought their own food and playthings. Might they follow us, so that I can look out for them and still enjoy Mary's picnic?"

Mrs. Howe smiled and said, "You are such self-reliant girls, and I admire that. But I think we can do a little better than having your sisters follow you. Why don't we simply invite them to enjoy our picnic? I'm sure we can manage to find enough food for everyone."

"That's very kind of you," Meg said. "But we have no desire to impose upon you."

"It would be no imposition at all," Mrs. Howe said. "Are those your sisters by the oak tree?"

"Yes, ma'am," Meg said.

"Tell them to come in," Mrs. Howe said. "I haven't seen them in so long, I shall need to be reintroduced."

Meg summoned her sisters. She could see how impressed they were by the splendor of the Howe house. Jo, Beth, and Amy each curtsied as Meg introduced them. Meg felt a flush of pride at how well her sisters were conducting themselves.

"The introductions are not yet complete, I think," Mrs. Howe said. "Beth, who is the young lady with you?"

Beth swallowed hard. It was painful for her to speak to people she did not know. "It's Emma," she said. "She had a terrible accident."

"I can see," Mrs. Howe said. "It's very kind of you to bring her along. I'm sure the sunshine will do her good."

Beth nodded.

"Meg, why don't you see how Mary is doing?" suggested Mrs. Howe. "I'll see to your sisters and to Emma. They look as though they're ready for an outdoor romp. And Willie is outside already. He'll be happy to have some playmates. Mary's room is the second door on the right upstairs. Come, girls. Let's see what games Willie has in mind."

Meg went upstairs, feeling almost sick with relief and excitement. She knocked on the second door and heard Mary invite her in.

"I've just finished dressing," Mary said. She had on a brown-and-white-checked cotton dress with a white pinafore. Meg had never seen such a pretty dress before except at church. She was wearing her gray school dress, which Marmee had assured her would be fine for a Saturday-afternoon picnic. "I'm glad you're early. Come, see my room."

Meg looked around. The room was filled with dolls and toys. And there was only one bed. Meg couldn't imagine how it would be not to share a room with her sisters.

"This is my favorite thing," Mary said, tak-

40

ing a little white-and-blue mug off a shelf. "My parents brought it from England for me. They go to Europe every year, you know."

Meg gently handled the mug. In blue letters it said, FROM YOUR AFFECTIONATE PARENTS.

"It's beautiful," she said, wishing her parents gave her similar gifts.

"Of course I have many finer things," Mary said. "Many of my dolls come from Paris and Dresden. The mug is really just a simple little thing. But when they gave it to me, Mama said if I was ever lonely for them, I could just look at the mug and remember how they love me. I don't suppose your parents travel very much."

"No," Meg said. "They did go to New York once."

"Sometimes I wish my parents didn't travel so often," Mary said. "But they do bring me lovely things. Come, let's go downstairs. I think I heard Sallie come in."

Meg cast one lingering look around Mary's room, trying to memorize it so that she could describe it to her sisters. Beth would be interested in the dolls, she thought, and Jo would

41

envy Mary her books. It was a splendid room, but Meg couldn't help thinking how lonely she'd feel in it, without her sisters to keep her company.

Priscilla had arrived with Sallie, and shortly thereafter, Willie's three friends came as well. Mary showed them all outdoors. Meg rejoiced that she was part of such a grand crowd.

CHAPTER 8

The Howes had a beautiful estate, filled with rosebushes and peonies. Meg immediately spotted Jo racing Willie across the field. Amy had already settled down with her drawing, and Beth was helping Emma sip some tea.

"Racing isn't very ladylike," Priscilla said as they watched Jo beat Willie by half a pace.

"Jo isn't very ladylike," Mary said. Willie's friends had joined Willie and were teasing him about losing to a girl.

"I let her win," Willie said. "Mama told me to. She never would have won otherwise."

"That's not true!" Jo cried. "I won fair and square."

Priscilla shook her head sadly. "And she uses such terrible slang," she said. "I'm never allowed to use slang."

"I'll race you again," Jo said. "I'll race all of you. Then you can see who the fastest runner is."

"I'm not going to race a girl," Freddie said.

"Come on, Willie," James said. "Don't you have any games just for boys?"

"I can play boys' games," Jo said. "I like to run and fight."

"Who invited her?" George asked. "I thought it was just four boys and four girls. I see seven girls."

"They invited themselves," Willie said. "And Mama said we had to take pity on them."

Meg thought she would die. Her cheeks turned bright red, and it was all she could do to keep from bursting into tears.

"Stop that, Willie," Mary said. "Mama never said anything of the sort, and you know it. Meg's sisters are as welcome here as your friends are. You're just angry because Jo beat you in the race. Come here, Jo, and play with us girls. We're going to play graces now. It's a much more ladylike game."

Meg held her breath. If she'd been embarrassed, she knew Jo was enraged. And an angry Jo could spoil everything for everybody, and she would not regret it until the following morning.

But Jo surprised her. "Graces will be fun," she said. "Meg and I play all the time at home."

Mary gave each of the girls a stick. She took a small hoop and tossed it. Priscilla caught it with her stick and then tossed it for Meg to catch.

Soon the girls were having a fine time trying to keep the hoop from falling to the ground. They were laughing so hard, the boys came over to see what kind of game they were playing. The boys even tried their hands at it, but the girls, who were more experienced, proved much better.

"What's that you're drawing, Amy?" Priscilla asked.

"A picture of Mary," Amy said.

"Oh, let me see," Mary said.

Amy, of course, needed no prompting. She displayed her picture with pride.

"It's really good," Mary said. "That looks a lot like me."

"Draw me next," Sallie said. "I've never had my portrait done."

"How about a game of battledore and shuttlecock?" Willie suggested. "Boys against the girls."

Everyone agreed. Soon the children were hitting the shuttlecock with their rackets, trying to keep it from falling to the ground. Each team had its share of successes and failures. Meanwhile Sallie sat posing as Amy sketched her, and Beth and Emma kept to themselves, contentedly watching the other children at play.

Everything was going splendidly when Meg felt a drop of rain against her cheek. By the time she'd looked up at the sky, another drop

had fallen, and another. In a moment the heavens opened, and the rain began falling heavily.

"Everyone inside!" Mary cried. "Girls, hurry, before your dresses get wet."

Jo won the race to the house easily. Meg stayed behind to help Amy and Beth gather their things.

"The picnic is ruined," Willie said. "Worse luck having it rain today."

"Now it's just a tea party," Freddie complained. "No fun at all."

"If they make us dance, I'm leaving," James said.

Meg sighed. Just when things had been going so well, the weather had to spoil everything. What a cursed picnic this was turning out to be.

CHAPTER 9

" *I*'ll see if the food is ready," Mary said. Meg thought Mary would run into the kitchen, but instead she pressed a bell and the butler appeared. Meg watched Amy's eyes grow large with excitement and envy.

"Is our meal ready?" Mary asked.

"I'm afraid not, Miss Mary," the butler replied. "We were told to serve at three."

"But that's not for another hour," Mary said. "What should we do until then?"

"Anything but dance," Freddie said.

"You have a piano," Meg said. "I noticed it

in your front parlor. Perhaps you could play, Mary."

"I don't know how," Mary admitted. "Mama says all truly cultured ladies should play the piano prettily, but I never have the patience to practice."

"Beth can play," Jo declared. "Beth makes the most wonderful music at home."

"A little girl like her?" Willie asked. "Playing our piano?"

"I'm sure it will be fine," said Mary. "Let's all go into the parlor and listen as Beth plays."

Beth cast a beseeching look at Meg. "Beth's shy," Meg said. "She isn't used to playing for strangers."

"You can do it, Bethy," said Jo. "Play the Stephen Foster songs we enjoyed the other evening."

"No one will laugh at me?" asked Beth.

"We won't let them," Jo said.

"Very well," Beth said with a sigh. She walked over to the piano. "Oh! It's so beautiful," she said. "It's so much lovelier than ours at home."

"But it has the same notes and plays the same songs," said Mary. "Can you play 'Jeanie with the Light Brown Hair'? That's my favorite."

"Yes, I know that one," said Beth. She sat down at the piano, a very little girl at a very grand instrument. Meg could see how nervous she was about even touching it. But then Beth pressed her fingers to the keyboard and out came the wonderful sounds of the Stephen Foster song.

"I dream of Jeanie with the light brown hair," sang Mary with great gusto. Soon the others had joined in.

"Beth, that was wonderful," Mary said. "What other songs do you know?"

"Beth knows lots of hymns," said Meg, hoping to help her sister out.

"Hymns are lovely," said Mary. "But it is Saturday and we are having a picnic, even if it is indoors. Beth, do you know any more songs by Stephen Foster?"

"She knows 'Oh, Susanna,'" Amy said. "That's my favorite."

"Mine too," said George. "Play 'Oh, Susanna,' would you, Beth?"

Beth began to play the song. Everyone joined in immediately.

Oh, no, thought Meg. Amy requested it so that she could do her little jig. The boys are sure to tease her if she does.

But Amy stood quite still and sang along in her childish soprano voice.

" 'Yankee Doodle,' " commanded Freddie when they had finished "Oh, Susanna." "Play 'Yankee Doodle' next. It's the perfect song for a picnic."

Meg worried that Beth didn't know "Yankee Doodle." They had never sung it at home, since most evenings they contented themselves with hymns. But much to her surprise and pleasure, Beth launched into "Yankee Doodle" without a moment's hesitation.

After that, Beth played "Camptown Races," "My Old Kentucky Home," "The Dying Sergeant," "Lord Randal," "Katy Cruel," "Barbara Allen," "Fiddle-De-Dee," and, at Freddie's insistence, another chorus of "Yankee Doodle." By the time the impromptu concert had ended, the children were ravenously hungry and in sparkling good spirits.

The meal only made them happier. It was a feast, with roasted chicken, asparagus fresh from the garden, mashed potatoes, sweet butter, and bread almost as good as the breads Hannah baked. Meg ate so much she thought she might never eat again, but, miraculously, when the ice cream and cakes appeared for dessert, she found herself eating as though she were starved. It was a feast she knew she would remember forever.

CHAPTER 10

*I*t continued to rain after lunch, and Freddie continued to grumble at the thought of dancing. Jo suggested charades instead.

"I'm not very good at charades," said Willie.

"Then we'll play on the same team," said Jo. "We play charades at home all the time, and I can help you with your turn."

Jo was as good as her word. She made no effort to dominate the game, but offered suggestions to Willie when he was assigned "Don Quixote" to act out. Willie's clues of *key, hoe,* and *tea* were regarded as brilliant by all present.

Amy, who enjoyed any opportunity to show off, begged to be included on Meg's team. She was given "To be or not to be" to act out and had great fun pretending to swat at a bee until her team guessed correctly.

Beth, who rarely played charades even at home, was given the task of assigning the titles to the competing teams. By game's end, Jo's team, with Willie, had won.

"That was capital!" said Willie. "I never knew one could have so much fun indoors with girls."

"Shall we play cards now?" Mary asked. "We have a deck for Old Maid and Old Bachelor."

"Are we allowed?" Beth asked Meg.

Meg was uncertain. They never played cards at home, since Marmee and Father regarded gambling as a sin.

"We don't play with a real deck of cards," said Willie. "It's a special deck just for children. Mama and Papa won't let us play with real cards."

"Then I'm sure it will be fine," said Meg, who wasn't sure at all but was too happy to worry about it.

Willie ran upstairs to get the cards. Soon he was teaching Jo the rules of the game and how best to play it.

Eventually the rain ended, and when it did, the first carriages appeared to take Sallie and Priscilla, then Freddie, James, and George, home. Meg and her sisters, of course, had no carriage and prepared for the long walk back to their house.

"Wait," said Mary as the March sisters began gathering up their belongings. "I want to give you something. It's in my room."

She ran up the stairs and came down with one of the dolls Meg had noticed earlier. "This is for you, Beth," Mary said, handing the doll over to her. "I have so many, I'm sure they don't get the proper attention. And you were so kind to play the piano for us. I don't know what we would have done without you. Yes, I do know. We would have fought and had a miserable time. That's what Willie and I do whenever it rains. Please take my doll and give her a good home. I'm sure she and Emma will learn to love each other."

"Thank you," Beth said. "But you really don't have to give me anything. I liked playing your piano."

"Take the doll," said Willie. "Mary has a roomful of them. She'll never notice it's missing. I only wish I had something to give you, Jo, for teaching me how to play charades."

"You could admit I beat you fair and square in our race," Jo replied. "None of your friends are here to make fun of you for losing to me."

Willie scowled. "You won't tell?" he demanded.

"It will be our secret forever," said Jo.

"You won fair and square," he said. "Mama never told me to let you win."

"Hurrah!" said Jo.

Meg gave her a look.

"That is to say, thank you," said Jo. "It was a fair race, and you ran it well. And you proved to be by far the best charades player."

"I *was* rather good," said Willie. "Perhaps you could come over some other time and we could play again."

"Perhaps," agreed Jo.

"I hope you will," Mrs. Howe said as she stepped into the parlor. "It was delightful having all the March girls here. Everything worked out for the best. The picnic wouldn't have been nearly as much fun without your sisters, Meg."

"Thank you for welcoming us," Meg said. "Now we really must be going." She remembered Marmee's instructions not to overstay her welcome. And that had been when she was the only guest from her family, as opposed to being one of four.

"I've arranged for our carriage to take you home," Mrs. Howe said.

"Oh, no, it's not necessary." Meg didn't see how she could accept any more generosity from Mary's mother. "We love to walk in the fresh air."

"Nonsense," said Mrs. Howe. "You're still our guests. Besides, the ground must be dreadfully wet from the rain."

"A carriage ride would be the perfect end to a most splendiferous day," said Amy.

"Yes, thank you, Mrs. Howe," said Beth. "And thank you again for the doll, Mary."

"Her name is Annabelle," said Mary. "She's from Paris, France."

"I'll speak French to her, then," said Beth. "When I learn it."

The children laughed together. Then Meg, having determined that her sisters had all their belongings, ushered them out the door and into the waiting carriage.

"What a wonderful picnic," said Jo as the carriage started rolling.

"Such delicious food," said Amy. "And all those servants. That's exactly how I'll live when I'm all grown up."

"Annabelle is the most beautiful doll I've ever seen," said Beth, who was carrying Annabelle carefully in her right arm while balancing Emma on her left. "Even so, I'm sure I'll learn to love her."

"Would you like me to tear off her arm?" Jo asked. "To make her feel more like part of the family?"

"No." Beth clung protectively to her newest baby. "At least, not just yet."

"Tell me when, then," said Jo, and joined in her sisters' laughter as they rode home through the streets of Concord.

CHAPTER 11

*A*s Meg awaited the return of Marmee and Father, she made a list of all the things she had done she was sure her parents would disapprove of. The list was long, and Meg wasn't sure how her parents would react when they heard it.

"Don't tell them everything," Amy suggested as she munched on a piece of bread and cheese. After the picnic meal, none of the girls was hungry for a real supper.

"I'm sure you could leave out the part about the cards," said Beth. "I don't think it was that great a sin, and I'm sure none of us will become gamblers as a result."

"No," said Meg sadly. "If I tell them one thing, I'll tell them everything. Otherwise I'll worry for the rest of my life that I'll let something slip."

"Do what you think best," Jo said. "Marmee is sure to notice that Hannah is missing, anyway."

"I hope she gets back soon," said Beth. "It's getting dark, and I wish somebody were here with us."

But Marmee and Father arrived home before Hannah. They had the look of people who'd spent a very pleasant afternoon visiting with good friends.

"How are my little women?" asked Father as he joined them in the parlor. "Were your picnics successful?"

"We worried when it started raining," said Marmee. "You did come in then, didn't you? Mrs. Howe must have seen to that, Meg, and Hannah must have tried to usher the rest of you girls indoors too. I hope you obeyed her."

"Speaking of Hannah, I'd enjoy a cup of

tea," said Father. "Amy, go into the kitchen and ask her to brew us some."

"Hannah isn't here, Father," Meg said.

"Where is she?" Marmee asked.

Meg looked at her sisters. "There are some things I need to tell you," she said to her mother. "May I speak to you in private?"

"Very well," said Marmee. "We'll go into the kitchen and make the tea."

Meg followed her mother into the kitchen and watched as she put wood in the stove to heat the water.

"Now," said Marmee. "Where is Hannah and what do you have to tell me?"

"Hannah's niece had her baby early," said Meg. It felt as if many days had passed since that announcement, instead of many hours. "Hannah left us alone so that she could take care of her niece and the baby."

"And you gave up Mary Howe's picnic to stay with your sisters?" asked Marmee. "Oh, Meg, how disappointed you must have been."

"That's not exactly what happened," Meg

replied, and soon she was telling Marmee the whole story. The confession took so long that the teakettle whistled just as Meg told Marmee about Annabelle the doll.

"My," said Marmee when Meg finally finished. "You really had quite an afternoon."

"It was wonderful," Meg said. "And it was terrible. There were a few moments when it was wonderful and terrible at the exact same time."

Marmee smiled. "That's just what growing up is like," she said. "Wonderful and terrible and sometimes both at the exact same time."

"I know I did wrong," said Meg, "but I'm not sure just how much wrong I did. And if I did a lot of wrong, then shouldn't I feel worse? Should I have enjoyed myself so if I was doing something bad?"

"The problem with doing bad things is that they can be very enjoyable at the time," Marmee said. "Otherwise we wouldn't do them—at least not so often."

"But you never do anything bad," said Meg.

"I try so hard to be like you, but there are so many temptations."

"Everything that tempts you has tempted me as well," said Marmee. "I'm no saint. I may never have played cards, but I have wasted whole afternoons on equally frivolous activities. And even your father has been known to go fishing at Walden Pond with no intention of bringing home dinner. He just wants the excuse to be outside with no obligations on a lovely summer day. We're none of us perfect, Meg. If we were, we would have nothing to strive for."

"I knew it was wrong for us to play cards," Meg said. "But if we'd said no, Mary would have been disappointed, and she'd been so kind to us all day."

"I think this once you can be forgiven," said Marmee. "But as you get older, people you think of as friends will offer you other temptations, and then you must find the strength to go against their wishes and say no. Remember how bad you feel now, having to tell me about the card playing. When you give in to temptation, there is always a price to pay."

"Mary was kind to us, though," said Meg. "And her mother was as well."

"It was very kind of Mrs. Howe to include your sisters in the festivities," said Marmee. "And when you write to thank her, I'll include a note of thanks myself. You do know, don't you, that you shouldn't have all gone there."

"I suppose," Meg said.

"Think of how you would feel if one of your friends did that to you," Marmee said. "Brought her three younger sisters along to a party you were giving."

"But it's different for us," Meg said. "We don't have very much money, and everybody knows that. The Howes are rich. They could afford the chicken and ice cream for all of us."

"That's no excuse for imposing on somebody's hospitality," Marmee said. "The right thing would have been for you to send Jo with a note to Mary explaining why you couldn't come, while you stayed home and tended to Beth and Amy."

"You're right," Meg replied. "I should have thought of that, but everything happened so suddenly, and I wanted to go to the picnic so much."

Marmee nodded. "It was a bigger sacrifice than you were willing to make," she said. "And, like the card playing, no real harm came of it. But your sense of shame must be very deep if you didn't want to tell all of this to your father."

"You're right," said Meg. "I am ashamed. But there's something else I want to ask you."

"What is that, dear?" Marmee asked as she checked the teapot.

"It's about Annabelle," Meg said. "Was it an act of charity for Mary to give it to Beth? Emma is so sorrowful looking with just one arm. I'm sure Mary thought that was the only doll Beth could afford. There were times today when I was sure Mary and her mother were being nice to us because they think of us as poor."

"Do you think of us as poor?" Marmee asked.

"Mary Howe owns so many things," Meg replied. "She owns twenty beautiful dolls, and Beth owns only six—counting Annabelle. But I'm sure there are children who don't even own that many. And I know there are children without a piano. Ours may be old and not very good, but we do own one. And we never go hungry or cold, and even if Amy does complain that all her dresses have patches, at least she has decent clothes to wear."

"Then we're not poor," said Marmee.

"We have only one servant, and our dishes are chipped," Meg said. "But Mary said on rainy days she and Willie always squabble. And some of our happiest days are when it rains and we play games inside and make up stories and work on our sewing together. And, Marmee, Jo and Beth and Amy all did what I asked them to do. When Jo was angry, she didn't storm; when Beth was shy, she played the piano; and Amy didn't thrust herself in the middle of everything and demand to be admired. Although, truth to tell, she got her share of petting anyway."

"And what does that say to you?" Marmee asked.

"That the love of my family is the greatest wealth I could have," Meg said.

"That's how your father and I feel," Marmee said. "Now let's bring the tea to your father before he sends out a search party for us!"

Meg nodded and helped her mother carry the tea things into the parlor. She smiled at the sight of the mismatched and chipped china cups. Her parents did not travel to Europe, but at least she had no need of a mug to assure her of their love.

Still, Meg thought as she looked at her family in the glow of early-evening candlelight, unchipped china and a roomful of dolls and scads of dresses and servants who came when you rang for them were all wonderful things in their own right.

"Bethy, play the piano," said Jo. "If you're not too tired from all the playing this afternoon."

"I could never tire of the piano," said Beth. "What would you like to hear?"

"Hymns," said Meg. "Play some hymns for us tonight."

Beth sat down at the piano. It had missing keys and a terrible tone. But to Meg's ears there was no sound so sweet as Beth's playing and the rest of her family singing hymns of thanksgiving for all the riches the March family had had bestowed upon them.

PORTRAITS OF
LITTLE WOMEN
ACTIVITIES

SCRUMPTIOUS
STRAWBERRY
SHORTCAKE

Generations of dessert lovers have enjoyed the simple and succulent combination of strawberries and cake. A tip: Strawberry shortcake is best eaten warm, so prepare it close to serving time.

INGREDIENTS

2-1/2 cups flour
2 teaspoons baking soda
1/2 teaspoon salt
1 tablespoon sugar
1/2 stick melted butter or margarine
1 egg
1/3 cup milk
2 pints ripe strawberries, washed and halved, plus more strawberries with hulls for garnish
Heavy cream, whipped and chilled (optional)

Preheat oven to 450 degrees.

1. Sift flour, baking soda, salt, and sugar into a bowl.
2. Add butter and mix until creamy.
3. Blend in egg and milk.
4. Place in an 8-by-8-inch Pyrex pan.
5. Bake in preheated oven 1/2 hour, until golden brown.
6. Remove cake from pan and cut into squares (any size you wish).
7. Place each cake square on serving plate and top generously with halved strawberries.
8. Place whole strawberry on top for garnish.

Serve with a dollop of whipped cream, if you wish.

Makes 9 to12 servings.

D R A W S T R I N G   B A G

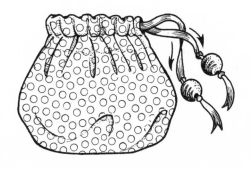

A drawstring bag is great for keeping barrettes, buttons, pins, or any other collection of small things.

MATERIALS
Ruler
Pencil
Paper (tracing or regular)
Scissors
Fabric, 16 by 9 inches
Straight pins
Thread
Needle
Safety pin
25-inch length of ribbon
2 macramé beads, 1/2 inch wide

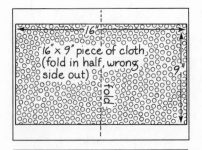

16"

16" x 9" piece of cloth (fold in half, wrong side out)

9"

fold

1. Using a ruler and pencil, draw a rectangle 6 inches wide and 7 inches long on paper. Cut out rectangle. This will be your pattern.

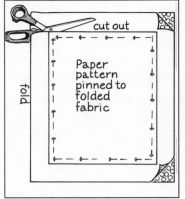

cut out

fold

Paper pattern pinned to folded fabric

2. Fold fabric in half with wrong side out. Pin pattern onto folded fabric and cut. Remove pattern.

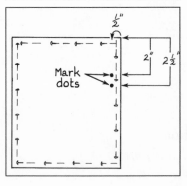

$\frac{1}{2}$"

2" $2\frac{1}{2}$"

Mark dots

3. Keeping the cutout fabric pinned together, mark two dots on wrong side of one piece of fabric—one dot 2 inches from top, the other 2-1/2 inches from top. Both dots should be 1/2 inch from edge. (See illustration.)

4. Cut a 20-inch piece of thread, and thread needle. Tie double knot at end.

5. Sew one short side and both long sides of bag together with a running stitch 1/2 inch from edge. (See illustration.)

6. Sew up to first dot, tie knot, and cut off extra thread. Start sewing from second dot to edge. Tie knot and remove pins.

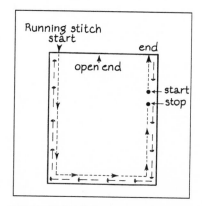

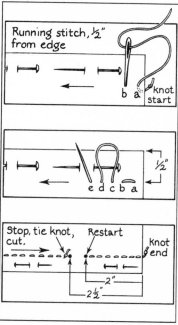

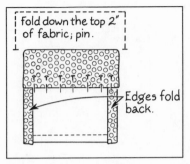

7. Fold top of fabric down 2 inches. (See illustration.)

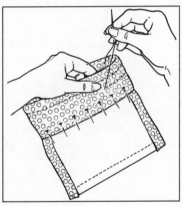

8. Sew a running stitch 1/2 inch from fold. Tie and knot. Sew another round of running stitches 1/2 inch below the first. Turn bag right side out.

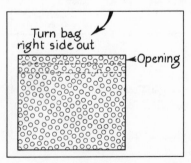

9. Tie one end of ribbon to end of a safety pin. Insert pin into the opening at top of bag and slide through to other end.

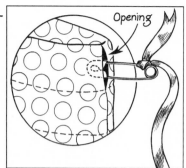

10. Remove safety pin. Tie knot in ribbon on both ends. Slip large bead onto each end and tie another knot.

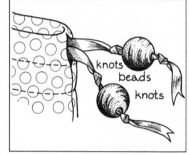

Now all you need to do is decide what to put in your drawstring bag!

Read all about Louisa May Alcott's
unforgettable heroines in
Portraits of Little Women:

Meg's Story

Jo's Story

Beth's Story

Amy's Story

Here are sneak peek chapters from each of
the other three delightful stories.

Jo's Story

CHAPTER 1

" Josephine! Josephine March!"

Jo March sighed and turned to face Aunt March. Only Aunt March called her Josephine and used that tone of voice.

"Yes, Aunt March?" she asked.

"What is that book in your hand?"

"It's *Oliver Twist*, Aunt," Jo replied. "By Charles Dickens."

"I know who wrote *Oliver Twist*, young lady," said Aunt March. "That book came off my shelves, did it not?"

"Yes, Aunt March."

"*Oliver Twist* is not suitable reading matter for a child," proclaimed Aunt March.

"I'm not so young," Jo said. "I'm ten."

"And a rude young girl, at that," Aunt March declared. "I sometimes wonder if your parents are teaching you manners."

"Father and Marmee are the best parents in the world," said Jo angrily. "Don't you speak against them."

"Don't you use that tone with me, young lady," Aunt March said. "Have your parents never taught you to respect your elders?"

"Of course they have," Jo said.

"Then the fault must lie with you."

"I'm sorry, Aunt March," said Jo, and she was sorry—sorry she'd aroused Aunt March's wrath, since it meant she'd be there for at least another ten minutes and would probably go home without the Dickens volume to read.

"I will never understand why you can't be more like your sister Margaret," said Aunt March. "Now, there's a girl your parents can be proud of. She's every inch a lady."

"Yes, Aunt March," Jo said. She tried to hide the copy of *Oliver Twist* in the folds of her skirt. "Meg is a lady."

"You could learn something from your sister Beth as well," said Aunt March. "Quiet as a church mouse and never causing any trouble."

"Yes, Aunt March," Jo said.

"Even little Amy could teach you a thing or two," said Aunt March. "She is such a darling child. Not at all the sort of child who talks back."

"Yes, Aunt March," Jo said for what felt like the hundredth time. Aunt March had a point. Meg was a lady—always polite, always willing to help others. Beth was a dear, sweet and kind. Amy was pretty and artistic, and even if she drove Jo to distraction, she was the sort of child Aunt March would favor.

And Jo was just the sort of girl that Aunt March would want to improve. Jo was sharp-tongued, quick-tempered, and boyish.

"I suppose your parents have done as good a job as they could raising you girls, having so little money and so many ideals," Aunt March declared. "Your sisters are a credit to them."

"I'll try to be better," said Jo.

Aunt March shook her head. "I've heard you make that promise a hundred times before, Josephine."

"It's hard," Jo blurted out. "Goodness comes so easily to Meg and Beth. And people always forgive Amy her mistakes because of her blond curls and pretty ways."

"You might not have Amy's curls," said Aunt March, "but couldn't you learn her ways?"

"No," Jo said, "I don't think I could."

Aunt March stared at Jo, and then, much to Jo's surprise, she laughed out loud. "I suspect you're right," she said. "Very well. You've paid your old aunt her visit. You may go home."

"Thank you, Aunt March," Jo said. She walked over to her aunt and kissed her cheek.

"But give me back *Oliver Twist*," said Aunt March. "If your parents approve of it for you, you may borrow it the next time you visit me."

"Oh, thank you, Aunt," said Jo, knowing that was far better than she could have hoped for. And the visit was over. It was all she could do to keep from skipping as she turned toward home.

Beth's Story

CHAPTER 1

"I do believe," Father March said, looking at his wife and their four daughters as they finished eating their supper, "that this is my favorite part of the day."

"Mine too," his second-oldest daughter, Jo, said. "It means school is over and so are our tasks."

"I like the mornings best," said Amy, the youngest of the girls. "The light is better then for drawing. Of course, in February there's hardly any light at any time of day. I like mornings best in the summer."

"I like midafternoon the best," Meg, the oldest, said. "Even on a cold winter's day. It's the warmest time of the day, and the sun shines the brightest."

"What about you, Bethy?" Marmee asked. "What is your favorite time of day?"

"I don't have a favorite," Beth replied. "It would be like having a favorite sister. Each is wonderful, and so is each time of day."

Marmee laughed. "I agree with Beth," she said. "Morning, noon, and night—they each have something to recommend them."

"And like your daughters, they each could stand a little improvement!" Jo said, and they all joined in her laughter.

"Nonetheless," Father said, "to sit here after one of Hannah's fine suppers, and to look at my wife and my four beautiful daughters—this is contentment of the purest kind."

"Notice how he puts supper first," Jo said. "Family comes after a full stomach."

"But the joy I get from my wife and daughters is a constant," replied her father. "And supper comes but once a day."

"He has you there, Jo," Meg said.

"But I fear this contentment will not last forever," said Father.

"Why not?" asked Beth, who was always fearful of change.

"He means we'll grow up," Meg said, "and marry and have families of our own."

"Not for a while, I should think," said Jo. "You're thirteen, Meg, and I'm twelve. I don't think Father approves of child brides."

"He said it wouldn't last forever," said Meg, "not that it was about to end next week."

"But next week is just when it will end," said Father.

His four daughters fell silent. Beth felt fear clutch her. Was Father going to leave?

"Your father is teasing you," Marmee said. She reached out to give Beth's hand a reassuring pat. "We're going to take a trip."

"A trip?" Jo asked. "Where to?"

"Your mother and I are going to New York City," replied Father. "We'll take the train there next week and stay for a week."

"How exciting!" Meg exclaimed. "Will you shop while you're there? Marmee, I hear the stores in New York are almost equal to those in London and Paris."

"And they're every bit as expensive," said Marmee. "I'll look around for bargains, but I doubt I'll find any. However, that's not the reason for the trip."

"What is, then?" asked Amy.

"There are several reasons, actually," Father said. "As you girls know, there is fear of a possible war in this country. The Southern states want to continue the expansion of slavery, and of course many of us in the North want slavery abolished altogether. Several of my friends here have asked me to go to New York to speak with some of the leading abolitionists, Mr. Horace Greeley and the Reverend Henry Beecher, for example, to determine what they think is likely to happen and to find out what we and they can do in the event of a war to see to it that slavery is finally ended."

"Mr. Greeley and Mr. Beecher!" Meg said. "They're so famous. Do you know them?"

"I've met them both, yes," Father said. "And we've exchanged letters recently. They agree it's a good idea for us to speak. This is an election year, and there are those who believe that if Mr. Lincoln is elected president, civil war will follow."

"And a jolly good thing it would be," said Jo. "I only wish I were a boy so I could fight for the rights of the slaves."

"War is never a jolly good thing, Jo," her father declared, "no matter how just the cause."

"So you'll be speaking to Mr. Greeley, and Marmee will be looking for bargains," Meg said. "It still sounds like a wonderful trip."

"It's more wonderful than that," Marmee said. "We'll be staying with my friend Mrs. Webster. Her daughter, Catherine, is engaged to marry a gentleman named Mr. Kirke."

"Are you going to the wedding?" asked Meg.

"I'm going to help prepare the trousseau," Marmee replied. "And to visit with my old friend. Mrs. Webster owns a boardinghouse, so there will be plenty of room for us to stay."

"And you'll be gone for a whole week?"

Beth asked. She knew she should be happy for her parents to have such an exciting trip planned, but she already missed them.

"A week," said Father. "Hardly enough time for all that's planned."

"What else will you be doing?" asked Amy.

"We want to go to the theater," Marmee said. "Edwin Booth is playing in *Hamlet*. And Mrs. Webster says we simply must see a production of *Uncle Tom's Cabin*. You know, the novel was written by Mr. Beecher's sister, Harriet Stowe. And what I think is most exciting of all, your father has agreed to have his photograph taken."

"Really?" Jo said.

"Mr. Emerson thinks it's a good idea," her father replied.

"And so do I," said Marmee. "I know I'll cherish a photograph of my handsome husband. And Mathew Brady, the most important photographer in this country, has consented to take the picture."

"What a week," said Meg. "The theater,

politics, a trousseau, Mathew Brady, and shopping!"

"I never thought Meg would put shopping last on her list of pleasures," Jo said, and they all laughed, even Meg.

"But there's one other thing to make it more perfect," said Father. "Your mother and I have gone over the expenses for the trip several times, and we agree that we can afford to take one of you along."

"Oh, take me, please!" cried Jo.

"No, me," said Amy.

"I should love it also," Meg said. "And I love to sew. I could help with the trousseau."

Beth only smiled.

"We suspected you would all want to go," said Marmee. "So we've decided to let you girls choose who will go to New York with us."

Beth looked at her sisters, all brimming with excitement. It would be a hard choice, but she knew whoever was selected would be the most deserving of the treat.

Amy's Story

CHAPTER 1

"What do you want most in the world, Amy?" Jo March asked her youngest sister.

It was a Saturday afternoon in April. There was a scent of springtime in the air, but it was too cold for Amy and her sisters, Meg, Jo, and Beth, to be playing outside. Instead they were in the parlor.

"Why do you want to know?" Amy asked.

"I was just wondering," Jo replied. "I know what I want: to be a famous writer. And Meg wants a husband and babies."

"I would like a husband and babies," Meg

said with a smile. "But not for another week or two, thank you. Right now what I'd like more than anything is a new dress. One I could wear to parties and not be ashamed of."

"You have nothing to be ashamed of," Beth said. "You dress beautifully, Meg."

Meg sighed. "Not compared to the girls I know. Anyway, that's what I want. A pretty new party dress."

"I want all of us to be happy," said Beth. "And some new sheet music. And a really fine piano. And a new head for my doll. Her headless body looks so sad."

"That's quite a list," Jo said. "Now, Amy, what's your pleasure?"

"A truly aristocratic nose," Amy replied. "You ought to know, Jo, since it's your fault I don't have one."

"Will you never let me forget?" Jo said. "I didn't mean to drop you when you were a baby. You must have been quite slippery."

"You couldn't be any prettier than you are now," Beth told Amy. "And I think your nose is extremely aristocratic."

"What else would you like?" asked Meg.

Amy thought about it. She knew she was pretty. Her shiny blond hair fell in lovely curls, and her eyes were as blue as cornflowers. Still, an aristocratic nose would help, but beyond sleeping with a clothespin on her nose there was little she could do to make it perfect.

"I'd like to be a real, professional artist," she said. "Someone who sells her paintings for lots and lots of money."

"I'd like that too," Jo said. "For you're a generous girl, Amy, and sure to share your wealth with your less fortunate sisters!"

The girls laughed. They were still laughing when their parents entered the parlor.

"What a wonderful greeting," Father said. "My little women enjoying themselves so."

"Father, Marmee!" the girls cried. They rushed into their arms and exchanged embraces.

"It is good to see you so happy," Marmee said. "Especially after the conversation we just had with the Emersons."

"Why, Marmee?" Beth asked. "Everything's all right with them, isn't it?"

"With them, yes," Father replied. "But not with the nation."

"You mean the Southern states seceding?" Jo asked. "President Lincoln will keep the country together. I'm sure of it."

"It will take more than words," said Father. "It was in the newspapers. The Confederates have fired upon Fort Sumter."

"Where's that, Father?" asked Meg. Amy was glad Meg had asked, as she didn't care to appear ignorant.

"It's in Charleston, South Carolina. The Union soldiers were asked to surrender but refused, and the Southerners fired upon them."

"How terrible," Meg said. "Were there fatalities?"

"Fortunately not," said Father. "But we'd be naive to think there won't be. War has begun, and there is always loss and suffering."

"I wish I were a boy," said Jo. "I'd enlist right away to fight for the end of slavery."

"I'm glad I have daughters and no sons,"

said Marmee. "It's selfish of me, but at least I don't have to worry about any of you dying in battle. No matter how noble the cause."

"You aren't going to go off to be a soldier, are you, Father?" asked Beth.

"I'm too old, I'm afraid," Father said. "All these years, I've fought for abolition, but what are words when young men are going to sacrifice their lives?"

"Words are what you have to offer," said Marmee. "And prayers too, for a quick resolution to this war."

War. Amy thrilled at the very word. She had no desire to be a boy and go off to fight. But, like Jo, she found the idea of war exciting. Handsome young men in uniform, fighting for a just and noble cause.

She supposed some of the men fighting for the South were handsome as well, but she didn't care. They were certain to lose and to realize how wrong they were.

"It's a good war, isn't it, Father?" she asked.

Father sighed. "All wars are evil. But in this case, there's a greater evil, and that's slavery.

So in some ways, it's a good war. But I pray it will be a short one, with little bloodshed."

"That's what we all should pray for," Marmee said.

Amy thought about her nose. It was selfish of her to wish for a nicer one when young men were going to risk their lives for the freedom of others.

"I'll pray for a short war, Father," Amy said. "And for freedom for the slaves."

Her father smiled at her. "I know you will, Amy. And I know my daughters will do everything they can to help the cause. Sacrifices will have to be made. But you'll do what you have to to alleviate the suffering of others."

"We will, I promise," said Meg. "We'll do whatever we can for the Union and for abolition."

Amy wondered what she would have to sacrifice. Anything but the clothespin, she thought, then realized she was still being selfish. Anything at all, she promised. She would sacrifice anything at all for the Union and abolition.

ABOUT THE AUTHOR OF
PORTRAITS OF LITTLE WOMEN

SUSAN BETH PFEFFER is the author of both middle-grade and young adult fiction. Her middle-grade novels include *Nobody's Daughter* and its companion, *Justice for Emily*. Her highly praised *The Year Without Michael* is an ALA Best Book for Young Adults, an ALA YALSA Best of the Best, and a *Publishers Weekly* Best Book of the Year. Her novels for young adults include *Twice Taken*, *Most Precious Blood*, *About David*, and *Family of Strangers*. Susan Beth Pfeffer lives in Middletown, New York.

A WORD ABOUT
LOUISA MAY ALCOTT

LOUISA MAY ALCOTT was born in 1832 in Germantown, Pennsylvania, and grew up in the Boston-Concord area of Massachusetts. She received her early education from her father, Bronson Alcott, a renowned educator and writer, who eventually left teaching to study philosophy. To supplement the family income, Louisa worked as a teacher, a household servant, and a seamstress, and she wrote stories as well as poems for newspapers and magazines. In 1868 she published the first volume of *Little Women*, a novel about four sisters growing up in a small New England town during the Civil War. The immediate success of *Little Women* made Louisa May Alcott a celebrated writer, and the novel remains one of today's best-loved books. Alcott wrote until her death in 1888.